The Nature of My Inheritance

BIBLIOMYSTERY SERIES

- #1 Ken Bruen, *The Book of Virtue,* $4.95
- #2 Reed Farrel Coleman, *The Book of Ghosts,* $4.95
- #3 Anne Perry, *The Scroll,* $4.95
- #4 Nelson DeMille, *The Book Case,* $6.95
- #5 C.J. Box, *Pronghorns of the Third Reich,* $4.95
- #6 William Link, *Death Leaves a Bookmark,* $4.95
- #7 Jeffery Deaver, *An Acceptable Sacrifice,* $5.95
- #8 Loren D. Estleman, *Book Club,* $4.95
- #9 Laura Lippman, *The Book Thing,* $4.95
- #10 Andrew Taylor, *The Long Sonata of the Dead,* $4.95
- #11 Peter Blauner, *The Final Testament,* $4.95
- #12 John Connolly, *The Caxton Lending Library & Book Depository,* $6.95
- #13 David Bell, *Rides a Stranger,* $4.95
- #14 Thomas H. Cook, *What's in a Name?,* $4.95
- #15 Mickey Spillane & Max Allan Collins, *It's in the Book,* $4.95
- #16 Peter Lovesey, *Remaindered,* $5.95
- #17 F. Paul Wilson *The Compendium of Srem,* $5.95
- #18 Lyndsay Faye, *The Gospel of Sheba,* $5.95
- #19 Bradford Morrow, *The Nature of My Inheritance,* $5.95

The Nature of My Inheritance

By

Bradford Morrow

Mysterious Bookshop

New York

The Nature of My Inheritance
by Bradford Morrow

Copyright © 2014

All rights reserved. Permission to reprint,
in whole or in part,
should be addressed to:
Otto Penzler
The Mysterious Bookshop
58 Warren Street
New York, N.Y. 10007
Ottopenzler@mysteriousbookshop.com

ISBN 978-1-61316-064-0 (Limited Edition)
ISBN 978-1-61316-065-7 (Paperback)

For Peter Straub

He that with headlong path
This certain order leaves,
An hapless end receives.

—Boethius,
The Consolation of Philosophy

The Nature of My Inheritance

*I*N THE WAKE OF MY FATHER'S DEATH, my inheritance of over half a hundred Bibles offered me no solace whatsoever, but instead served to remind me what a godless son I was and had always been. Like the contrarian children of police officers who are sometimes driven to a life of crime, and professors' kids who become carefree dropouts, my father's devotion to his ministry might well have been the impetus behind my early secret embrace of atheism. In church, listening to his Sunday sermons, as I sat in a pew with my mother near the back of the sanctuary, I nodded approvingly along with the rest of the congregation when he hit upon this particularly poignant scriptural point or that. But in all honesty, my mind was a thousand light years away, wallowing, at least usually, in smutty thoughts.

His last day in the pulpit, his last day on earth, was no different. I cannot recall with precision what lewd scenario I was playing out in my head, but no doubt my juvenile pornography, the witless daydream of a virgin, did not make a pretty counterpoint with my father's homily.

Why he bequeathed all these holy books to me wouldn't take a logician to reckon. My mother spelled it out in plain English when we were in the station wagon, along with my little brother, Andrew, heading home after the funeral, and she broke me the news about my odd inheritance. "He worried about you day and night, you know. He thought you should have them so you might start reading and find your path to the good Lord."

I didn't want to sound like the ingrate I was, so suppressed my thought that a single Bible would have been more than sufficient.

"Take care of them, Liam," she continued. "Do his memory proud."

"I'll try my best," I said, trying to sound earnest.

"And never forget how much he loved you," she finished, her eyes watering.

"I won't, ever," I said, in fact earnest, praying she wasn't about to crash our car into a curbside tree.

My mom was a good soul and her intentions were every bit as virtuous as my father's. Both of them were delusional, though, to think I was going to sit in my attic room, put away my comics, set aside my Xbox, turn off my television, and switch over to Genesis. I was fourteen back then, though I looked older, was recalcitrant as a wild goat, locked in a losing battle with raging hormones I didn't understand, and while I was capable of barricading myself behind a bolted door to read every banned book I could lay my hands on, I wasn't about to launch into the Scriptures. To please my poor distraught mother, I did make the gesture of moving the unwanted trove of Bibles up to my room, where I double-shelved them alongside *Catcher in the Rye*, *Candy*, *Lady Chatterley's Lover*, and the rest of my more profane paperbacks.

To my eye, the Holy Books were ugly monstrosities, all sixty-three of them, bound variously in worn black leather with yapped edges, frayed buckram in a spectrum of serious colors, tacky over-ornamented embossed leatherette. Most of them were bulky, bigger than my own neglected, pocket-sized copy, and as intimidating in their girth as they were in their content, tonnages of rules and regulations from on high, miles of begets and begats. I was fascinated that a dozen of them were bound in hard boards fastened shut with brass or silver clasps that needed a key to open. I would have to look for the keys sometime, I supposed, but since I had no intention of reading them, there was no rush to go hunting around the house. The whole passel of stodgy books contained the same basic words, the same crazy fairy tales, anyway, so what did I care?

It needs to be said at the outset that my father, the Reverend James Everett, minister at the First Methodist Church of —, did not die from natural causes. He was as hale as he was old-school handsome, with cleft chin, distinguished wavy hair, and the coral-cheeked glow of an adolescent rather than a man well into his forties, the result of clean living and a lineage of parents, grandparents, and great-grandparents, all of whose middle names were Longevity. He never smoked, not even a pensive evening pipe. He drank exactly one glass of rum-spiked eggnog every year before Christmas dinner, which brightened his cheeks all the more, but other than that and maybe a taste of communion wine, he was as abstinent as Mary Baker Eddy. In winter he shoveled our walk and our next door neighbors' in his oversize shearling coat, and in summer mowed our lawn—me, I was relegated to weeding my mother's flower garden—wearing a white short-sleeve shirt, clip-on bowtie, and straw boater hat. He was an exercise nut who did a hundred sit-ups every morning and a hundred push-ups before bed. Above all, my father loved walking. He walked here and walked there, and for longer distances, much to my embarrassment, rather than drive the family station wagon, a relic that dated back to the Triassic, he rode a bicycle, his back as straight as Elmira Gulch's in *The Wizard of Oz*—except with a faint smile on his face rather than her witch's frown. He was slim as a reed and wiry as beef jerky. Some of my friends thought he was a bit of a dork, and while I didn't argue, I knew that if he and any of their dads stripped down to the waist and squared off, my father would pummel them to pulp.

He seemed to have no enemies, my pop. It was safe to say, or so all of us thought, that he was one of the most liked and respected people in the whole town. All who knew him, whether they were members of his congregation or not, from councilmen who sought his support during elections to pimply grocery boys who happily sacked his free-range steaks and organic greens, agreed that my father was never meant to die. My flaxen-haired and walnut-eyed Sunday school teacher, Amanda was her name—a name that rightly meant "worthy of love"—confided in me when I was ten or eleven, "Your dad is too good to go to hell, and too useful to the Lord's work here to go to heaven." I think that was one of the few times in my life I felt sorry for him, a wingless angel with eternal chewing gum on the soles of his shoes that allowed him a future in neither some balmy paradise nor a roasting inferno. Since I didn't believe in hell or heaven, though, my sorrow quickly dissipated, was replaced by a mute chuckle, and soon enough I was back to wondering what gently curvy, sweet-spirited Amanda, in her late teens, looked like when she changed out of her clothes for bed.

And yet for all I looked down my freckled nose at my reverend father's zealous and traditionalist beliefs, I missed him at the dinner table, saying the same dull prayer before every meal, passing me and my brother the meat, vegetable, and starch dishes my mother cooked every night. I missed him carefully reading our school papers and suggesting areas for improvement. I missed his attempts at being a regular-Joe father who took his sons to college football games and sat during our annual excursion to the Jersey shore under a beach umbrella while Andrew and I screeched and splashed around in the water, wrestling in the frothy green breakers. Above all, I missed his warm fatherly presence, like a fast-growing, scraggly rose vine might miss its fallen trellis, despite the fact I had gone out of my way, especially in recent years, to be a thorn in his side.

At the funeral, a hundred mourners converged, and I couldn't help but overhear the rumors about what might have caused him to fall down the set of hardwood stairs that led from the church chancellery to the basement after giving a powerful sermon, by their lights anyway, about the iniquity of avarice and the blessed nature of giving. I knew the message of this sermon well, to the point of nausea honestly, as he and my mother discussed it after dinner for a solid two weeks before he stepped into the pulpit and delivered it on that doomed day. Living in the household of a church father means, for better or worse, having certain insights into the mechanical workings, the practical racks and pinions, of what transpires behind the ethereal parts of any ministry. See, being a clergyman isn't all riding around on puffy clouds and giving godly advice and just generally being a beacon of hope and inspiration. It is about keeping the tithes and offerings flowing, like mother's milk—oh, Amanda—so staff wages can be paid, the church roof doesn't leak, the stained glass window that some local punks saw fit to riddle with thrown rocks can be repaired. The church is a nonprofit, so the tax man never came knocking, but the insurance man did, as well as many others whose services were necessary to keep the ark afloat and the fog machine running—at least, that's how I viewed things from my corner perch in the peanut gallery, knowing leather-winged Lucifer waited for me with open arms in the bowels of Hades.

Simply and seriously put, my father was in desperate need of money. Utility bills were overdue. Last year's steeple restoration remained largely unpaid. The organ was in serious need of an overhaul, and while it had sat idle for a year or so, the piano that replaced it had steadily gone out of tune. Even his own stipend was at risk. I am sure that for every single problem I knew about, watching my folks wringing their hands on a nightly basis and sharing dire worries, there were ten more deviltries utterly unknown to me. One night, when I wandered in on them, deliberately, I must admit, although pretending I only just then heard about these money issues, I offered to pick up a job after school to help out.

"That's good of you, Liam," my father said. "But I don't think you understood what we were talking about. No need for worry, everything's perfectly fine. You just stick to your schoolwork and our lord savior will take care of the rest."

Yes, he often spoke in such ecclesiastical terms. If it weren't so innocently offered, his dimples flexing from nervousness and earnest blue eyes searching for the confidence their owner so badly wanted to convey to his eldest son, I would have snorted, "Please, spare me!" Or, worse, I would simply have laughed. I did neither but left the room knowing that I had tried to intercede and was rejected. Like a latter-day Pontius Pius, if a lot more reluctantly, I washed my hands of the matter.

No one at the funeral said that my father was pushed down the stairs, not in so many words. Nobody whispered that he had borrowed himself into debt, very deep debt, on behalf of the church, not in so many words. And not one soul suggested in so many words that in order to get these loans, the church's minister found himself dealing with less than savory elements in the community, churchgoing, god-fearing folks, maybe, but people for whom the less-than-flattering term "elements" was intended nonetheless. The rumormongers were vaguer than all that. It was from their overheard tones of voice that I cobbled together what I knew, or thought I knew, they were huddling about. One can say the phrase "He's such a good boy" so that it means *the boy is good* or *the boy is bad* just by intoning it differently. That much I understood, as I wandered around, shadowed by my brother, for whom our abrupt fatherlessness hadn't yet sunk in fully, accepting people's condolences, not trusting a single one of them, looking into their eyes for a confession of some kind. I wasn't any more in my right mind than Drew, though I felt I needed to put a brave face on my stunned confusion. The way I figured it was that my father was in the peak of health, athletic in his way, cautious of diet, regular of habits, head on his pillow at ten, up with the cock's crow at six. In church business he might have been stumbling, but when walking down that flight of stairs after his sermon that Sunday he did not trip, that much I felt was irrefutable.

The coroner wasn't so sure. While there was no evidence of a heart attack or anything else in the autopsy to suggest that he had collapsed or fainted, the theory was floated that my father had simply slipped. To me that made no sense, as he had descended those well-lit stairs thousands of times, and while some structural elements in the rest of the church might have needed repair, the hardwood treads on that staircase didn't even creak, let alone give. For me, it wasn't his health, wasn't those stairs, and don't even hint at suicide. Christ was far more suicidal than my dad. No, I knew in my heart that my father was shoved to his death. The sole problem with my theory was that no one else had been seen back in the stairwell at the time, no one witnessed his tumble or heard him cry out. The unimaginable sound of his skull cracking open, maybe like the cantaloupe he distractedly dropped on the kitchen floor that morning as he carried it from the refrigerator to the counter, was one I did my level best to self-censor. I kept reminding myself about the tree that falls in the forest with no one there to listen, and how it makes no sound. Pathetic, but I found myself in a completely foreign emotional terrain and was forced to improvise the best I could. Lying awake at night, my game console lost on me, my small television muted although I left the picture on for company, I sleuthed my way through every person I had seen with my father during the last months, trying without luck to identify a possible culprit.

A detective had dropped over the Sunday afternoon of my father's death to ask my mom, who was numb with heartache and barely able to process his queries about whether her husband had any disagreements, arguments, altercations with anybody. When he stopped by again, not a week later, I knew something was afoot.

"I'm very sorry about your loss," he said, repeating his words from that prior visit.

"Thank you," my mother said, repeating hers.

"I wonder if you wouldn't mind going over a few things with me, now that a little time has passed—"

"We only just buried him," she countered, then immediately apologized. "Anything you need. Liam, you should go upstairs."

"No, that's all right," said the detective. "Nothing to hide here. Plus, maybe he'll know something, right? Liam, is it?"

"Yes, sir," I said, all military and respectful for some reason. Badge was unshaven and wearing a pale gray hoodie, a countercultural cop as I saw it, which made me like the man, gave me confidence that a regular blue uniform wouldn't have. There was something familiar and comfortable about him, too. I was no more fond of police than I was of clergymen, my father excepted, but this one with his frayed jeans was copacetic, in my book.

He did ask many of the same questions as he had before when I listened in from the adjacent room. Had my father counseled any domestic violence couples or individuals prone to aggressive behavior and happened to mention that he had been threatened as a result? Had she or the deceased—I hated hearing my father called that—seen anybody unusual lurking around the church premises, anybody who wasn't part of the regular community of worshippers? Had there been any peculiar phone calls, or calls at odd hours? Any menacing letters at home or the church?

My mother gave him the same answers as the first time, but when he got around to asking again if any of the church employees had been fired or cut back on their paid working hours, she interrupted, "Well, wait. You know, we were getting some calls late at night this fall, around Halloween."

"What kind of calls?"

"I couldn't say, really. The reverend always took them, given the hour, and when I asked him who was it, he told me it wasn't anybody and just to go back to sleep."

My mother always referred to my father as the reverend. Others thought it somewhat peculiar, but I was used to it from as far back as I could begin to understand language itself, so to my ear it was second nature, even first nature.

"And what did you do then?"

My mother looked confused by the question. "I went back to sleep."

"Did you ask about it in the morning?"

"No, there was breakfast to make, the boys to get off to school, and all the rest. Since he made no big deal about it, neither did I."

The detective pressed, gently. "How many times would you say these middle-of-the-night anonymous calls happened?"

"Maybe half a dozen or so. And I never said they were anonymous, just that the reverend never told me who it was."

Out of the blue, the detective turned to me and asked, "How are you holding up, son?"

"I'm good, I guess."

"You helping your mother out, I imagine?"

"I'm trying," I said, wondering why he would ask me such lame questions. "You know he was murdered, my dad, right?"

His turn to be taken aback a little. "We don't have any solid evidence to suggest that he was. Chances are, this was a tragic accident. He took a misstep and fell. Sad to say it does happen. Accidents are far more common than murders."

"He was murdered," I said, looking at him coolly in the eyes. "I know it."

"Liam," my weary mother admonished me.

"No, that's okay," said the detective. "Since we're not sure what happened yet, he has every right to his opinion. We'll see about looking into those late night calls, if there's any record of them. Meantime, if you think of anything, you already have my cell number, so call me any time," he finished, rising to go. I saw him to the door and walked him out to his unmarked dark blue Chevy. On the sidewalk, he asked me, "Between you and me, Liam, why is it you think your dad was murdered? A hunch or what?"

I weighed whether to tell him about all the people to whom my father owed money, all those who were waiting patiently for the church to raise enough to clear its debts, and all those who were less than patient. But I assumed he and the rest of the authorities were already aware about this darker side of my father's goings-on and were looking into it even as we stood there.

"You know," I said, unhelpfully, "sometimes you just know."

Looking back, I know he knew that I knew nothing.

The famous old biblical phrase, *An eye for an eye, a tooth for a tooth*, circulated in my mind like an endless loop in the days that followed the detective's visit to our house. For reasons I could not then explain to myself, it lodged in my dreamy head with such sticky vengeance that even my fantasy thoughts about Amanda—who visited us several times in the wake of the reverend's death, a demure young woman behind whose shy gaze I swore lay an unawakened erotic soul—were pushed to one side of my streaming consciousness. This new obsession, a vehement, dry mania rather than an amorous, damp one, was upsetting on many counts. I far preferred Amanda to Leviticus, but the latter had me in its Old Testament clutches. So much so that I decided to put one of my father's Bibles to use, research where that line came from and exactly what it meant, though I suspect my father wouldn't have approved of his eldest son's deepening desire for justice in the form of revenge if and when the perp was found.

Even though it would have thrilled my mother to see me sitting with a King James, leafing through its chapters and verses in search of this charming retribution adage, I had my pride and independence to uphold, and so waited for the lights in our house to go off and my family, all two of them, to fall asleep. As I thought before, when I first inherited these big fat tomes, one Bible was the same as the next, and so I pulled down the first that came to hand. It was on the medium-sized side, a pebbly, limp leather binding sheltering the holy words, but when I looked at the title page and saw it was printed in some language I didn't know, German I think, I shut it without looking further and reshelved the thing. Why would my otherwise rational, bow-tied, lawn-mowing dad bequeath me a damn Bible in German, or whatever foreign language that was? Maybe he had gone a little more mental in these last years than I'd thought.

Next I chose one of the larger volumes, since it read *Holy Bible* on the spine in good old-fashioned English. Settling it on my lap as I sat on the edge of my bed, I opened it up to the table of contents for the Hebrew scriptures—I was a methodical fellow, being Methodist, see—and ran my finger past Genesis and Exodus to Leviticus where, after reading around for a while, I found my phrase. Commentary at the bottom of the page confirmed that the maxim meant exactly what it sounded like. Whoever has inflicted an injury must suffer the same injury in order for justice to be served. Leviticus 24:20 cross-referenced me back to Exodus 21:24 which cross-referenced me to Deuteronomy 19:21— these Old Testament types, I thought as I shook my head, were all on the same page when it came to punishment. Then I was referred forward to Matthew 5:21, where, as I knew from my father's frequent references to the verse, stern Old Testament practicality was replaced by the gentler love-your-enemies philosophy of the New Testament. Since I believed in none of this nonsense, I suppose it didn't matter that I sided with the fire-and-brimstone crowd, especially in the wake of my father's abrupt, inexplicable death and maybe fueled by some of the fiercer among my Xbox games. So I decided to see what argument gospeler Matthew might make to convince me otherwise, and opened the Bible about halfway through.

What I encountered made my jaw drop. Right in the middle of the Bible somebody had carefully carved out a secret compartment that couldn't be seen when the book was closed. Hundreds of pages were vandalized, if that was the word for it, in order to hollow out the block of paper just enough to fit inside its dry bowels yet another book. Having no idea what I was doing or what I had stumbled upon, I lifted out the volume that was nestled like an unholy fetus inside the Bible. I set the Bible aside and held this smaller book, as careful as if it were a new alien species and I happened to be the scientist who discovered it, up to my astonished eyes.

The book was in Latin, which was better than German, since I had spent a grueling year in junior high school trying to learn it, for no meaningful reason I could see until now. Using my rickety knowledge of that defunct tongue, I made out that this pretty pocket-sized book was printed in 1502, by one Aldo Manuzio, in Venice. I was fascinated by the image of a dolphin wrapped around an anchor on the last page, but only got truly excited—so excited I started wheezing and had to use my inhaler—when I Googled around and learned that what I had found inside my father's Bible was the first Aldine edition, as it was called, of Dante's *The Divine Comedy*. That, in and of itself, wasn't the source of my shortness of breath and whistling windpipes, though. As my eyes scrolled down the backlit screen of my tablet, I learned that this was one of the most important books in the history of printing, the first of Aldo Manuzio's literary titles available to the regular public, groundbreaking because its revolutionary format made it as portable as one of my risqué paperbacks. And it didn't hurt my opinion of the thing that, five hundred years later, it was worth over twenty thousand dollars.

Mind-blown, rattlebrained, heart pounding in my ears, my first thought was where I should hide this treasure, before realizing that the best place to stow it out of sight was right where I found it. After tucking it away again, a golden Jonah safely back in its whale belly, and sliding it onto the shelf, I slipped the tablet under my pillow and turned off the bedside light. Out my dormer window was a crescent moon that looked like a cockeyed smile, probably like the smile on my face as I lay there mulling over my miraculous find. My dear Amanda, light of my life, fire of my loins—yes, to be sure, I had tried and failed to read *Lolita*—lost out to Dante Alighieri as the center of my focus that night while I drifted off toward sleep, my thoughts bubbling and stewing in a cauldron of questions desperate for answers.

Next morning, fearing the whole thing had been a dream, I checked to see if Jonah was still there inside his squarish whale. That he was came both as a relief and a worry. The relief was obvious. Twenty-thousand reasons why and then some. But the worry was, what now? How was it that my father possessed such a valuable book, secreted away like that?

My mother commented when I staggered into the kitchen, "Liam, your eyes are all bloodshot. You feeling sick?"

"Not so great, Mom," I said without a moment's thought, slumping down in my chair at the breakfast table.

"Maybe you better stay home from school today. It's cold out and I don't want you catching a flu bug."

If I had written the script, I wouldn't have changed a word.

"I want to stay home, too," my brother tried, a bit over-eager.

"Why in heaven's name should you stay home?" our mother asked with a mild scowl, as she forked some toaster waffles onto our plates. "You're not sick."

"Yes, I am," he said, offering his audience what was easily the most fake cough anybody ever made in the entire recorded history of humankind.

Laughter hadn't been heard much in our household those days, so the sound of it, loud and infectious cackles and snorts, was jarring at first. When Drew, knowing his gambit had flamed, broke down laughing, too, I felt as if things were eventually going to be okay for us and that life would hobble on.

Among the very first things my mother told me, after she gave me the calamitous news about Dad, was, "Now you're going to have to be the head of the family and take your father's place in whatever ways you can. He would want you to be responsible and mature enough to do that, Liam." At the time, while I nodded and said I would do her as proud as I could, my fantasy was that Amanda would move in with us as my wife, and Drew and Mom would be like our children. Something along those lines. The implausible reverie didn't linger longer than an August icicle.

Now, though, as our laughter died down, I did sense I might be on the right path to assuming the role she described, wearing the pater's pants, despite the fact that I was faking illness to ditch school like some punk third grader. It was a necessary ploy, though. I wanted time to think. Time to ponder what to do.

Needless to say, I couldn't wait for my family to leave so I could have the house to myself. I traipsed upstairs, my glass of grape juice in hand—the reverend bought bottles of this by the case; we were all addicted to the stuff—and pretended to go back to sleep. When my mother checked on me, I offered her the comfort of finding her sick son safely dozing in bed. I even managed to twitch a little as if I were dreaming, just to add to the effect. She said nothing, although I felt I could plainly hear her thoughts, *Poor child's been through the wringer, immune* system's off-kilter, good for him to have a day off to rest. After I heard her walk back downstairs, open and close the front door, and drive off in the station wagon with Drew, I swung my legs out of bed and in my pajamas dashed to my parents' bedroom where I easily found a sock stuffed with the keys to the locked volumes in the top drawer of my father's dresser. Not the most canny hiding place anybody ever came up with, but that was him all over again. I wasted no time chasing back to my room and unlocking the first Bible that came to hand.

The hidden book this time was from the fifteenth century, Boethius's *De consolatione philosophiae*, in chestnut colored leather, very plain Jane. It was so rare, or so it seemed, that I couldn't even find a copy offered for sale by any book dealer online and, not knowing as yet how to locate auction records, had to conclude the thing was basically priceless. I marveled at its text, not a line of which I could read, and at its agelessness, these words written in 524 AD or thereabouts, according to my research, while this Boethius, about whom I knew nothing before that morning, was in jail for treason, brought to his knees by yellow-belly treachery. In other words, an outlaw I could get behind. His book seemed to make a bunch of nods to god, but really was a chat with the beautiful Lady Philosophy—Amanda's face floated into view—about how fame and fortune melt away, about how all of us are good inside even though we do wrong things, about how prisoners should be treated with kindness by their captors, about how god doesn't finally run things but men of free will do. Awesomeness incarnate, I thought. I could have spent the whole rest of the term in school twenty-four-seven and not learned as much as I did that morning, sitting with what I began to wonder wasn't just maybe a stolen Boethius and chewing over what my father was doing with it in his possession, not to mention the other concealed rarities I found.

With the exception of one, which I guessed the reverend used to read from, not a single solitary Bible I inherited wasn't hollowed out with a rare book secreted inside. I found out they were called smuggler's Bibles, and were used in the old days for a purpose that wasn't much different than what my dad seemed to be using them for. It was pretty smart of the old man, smarter than I suppose I'd have given him credit for knowing, that if you wanted to hide something in a place nobody would bother looking, a good old Bible was perfectly suited to the task.

I started making a list of titles and a tally of

market values, aware that my phony cold would have to worsen over the next couple of days so I would have time to finish the job. Since I rarely got sick and had a real excuse for coming down with something—exhaustion from the shock of losing my dad—my mother was lenient about letting me continue to stay home from school that week. My poor brother, who saw right through my hoax, writhed with jealousy. But there wasn't a thing he could do, especially after that bogus cough of his became a running joke at mealtimes. So I tucked the aspirin and cold medication pills in my cheek, just as I had seen in the movies, drank water from the glass my mom handed me, swallowed mightily, then spat out the pills onto my palm the minute she turned her back. I managed to drink hot tea on the sly before she put the thermometer in my mouth to take my temperature, and the results were impressive. Part of me wished I had played this game of charades earlier, but I knew my father would have called me out in a heartbeat, laid a choice line of scripture on me about lying, and that would have been curtains, no encore.

But what about him and lying? Or, if not lying, keeping a secret from his family to the tune of half a million plus for starters—these books added up fast, reaching into six figures even before I was a quarter of the way through the trove. Just for example, the first edition in English, 1640, of Niccolò Machiavelli's *The Prince*, which I learned was the greatest textbook of all time for political leaders interested in wielding power with an iron fist, brought in the neighborhood of sixty grand or more. Little brat of a book, too, a duodecimo they called it. Or what about Voltaire's *Candide*, one of a dozen or so copies of what was known as the quote-unquote true first edition, published in Geneva in 1759? A sheaf of fussy notes about its "points" that verified it as legitimate was tucked into the smuggler's part of the Bible underneath *Candide* itself. Online, a British book dealer—I wondered if they ought to call themselves bookies?—had one of these for £60,000, which the conversion chart made out to be about a hundred thousand dollars just by itself. It went on like that. Mary Shelley's *Frankenstein* in three small volumes hidden in three different Bibles, the 1818 first edition? Worth a hundred and a half, easy.

But what on earth was my dad, the good reverend, doing with *Frankenstein* when he wouldn't even let me and Drew see the movie because he didn't want our snow-pure souls corrupted by the spectacle of a half-man, half-monster roaming around terrorizing people and drowning little girls? Though he never found out, we did see the James Whale original on a friend's computer, harmless enough moth-bait relic that it was, but the more I thought about *Frankenstein*, Boethius, Machiavelli, and the rest, the more I realized that my father and I couldn't be the only ones who knew about the pearls inside these oysters. Couldn't be blind to the fact that his murder probably had to do with all this. Problem was, if I talked to the detective about it, I worried that the authorities might take my books away from me. But if I didn't, then whoever pushed my dad down the stairs might never get caught.

Late morning on the third day of my convalescence—where was Amanda Nightingale when her fallen soldier needed succor?—the telephone rang. This threw me way off, since the house had been quiet as a toothache during the first two days. I debated whether to answer. If I did and it was my mother checking up on me, she might say if I'm well enough to talk on the phone I'm well enough to go to school. Ixnay to that, since I needed at least one more day to finish going through the Bibles. On the other hand, what if it was that detective who maybe had a lead or something? Damned if I did, damned if I didn't, so damn it I did.

"Everett residence," I half-croaked, in case it was the mater.

"Who's this?" was what the man on the other end asked.

I'm not the epitome of etiquette, not by a muddy mile, but that struck me as rude.

"Who is this?" as breezy as I could muster now that I knew it wasn't my mother.

"Is Reverend Everett there, please?"

"This is his son. And who, may I ask, is calling?"

Bread on the water, see.

"I need to speak with the reverend himself, I'm afraid, on a private matter. Would you mind letting him know there's a party on the phone who wishes to speak with him?"

Just as the decision whether or not to pick up this call was a kind of crossroads, I found myself at another crossroads here. Do I tell him about my dad's demise, or play out the line a little more, see what this was about?

"He's not here right now. If you give me a name and number—"

And he hung up. Needless to say, as I continued to work on cataloguing, and roughly, very roughly, appraising the books inside the books as best I could, recognizing my limitations and at the same time continuing to marvel at the literary gems I unearthed, the dark cloud of that call hung over me. Seldom the nervous type, except in the presence of Amanda, whose mild voice raised sweat on my palms and soft scent made my heart race, every lousy sound I heard downstairs, when the furnace boiler went on or the hall clock struck the hour, caused me to jump. I didn't like that man on the horn. I didn't like that my father had left me with such a weird legacy. I didn't like it that my earlier little-boy judgment about my dad's death being a murder had now transformed into my not-so-little-anymore son's conviction that I had been dead-on right. I looked at the confounding array of books, as many of them as worthless as the others were valuable, and shook my head in wonder and despair. If the reverend were here, as I very much wished he were, he would no doubt have had some catchy proverb to impart, some elegant verse from the Bible that would bring this mess into focus and help my suddenly incomprehensible world make sense.

"Where are you, man? What's all this mean?" I asked and, ashamed as I am to admit it, began crying.

Toggle life back to summer. Hot as skeet, sky the color of a tin can, the air murky as math. My father and I together in the wagon with its fake wood panels and shocks so spongy every pothole made us heave and bounce like a rowboat on rolling waves. We were headed over to the church with some hymnals another ministry was kind enough to donate, or re-donate, to the First Methodist church. Brotherly-love sort of gesture in the "Give and it shall be given unto you" tradition. It was pretty nice of them, since our church, whose lower middle-class congregation was strong in faith but feeble when the collection plate was passed around, had nearly run out of hymnals. Guess some people wanted to take them home so they could sing all the verses of "The Old Rugged Cross" in the comfort of their bathrooms.

I helped the reverend, who was in an off mood that late August day, take the boxes of chunky hymnaries out of the car and into the church, where he had me unpack and tuck them into the book racks behind each pew while he went downstairs to his office. Off, too, was that he palmed me two dollars and told me to head over to the bodega a few blocks away and get myself a soda or candy or whatever I wanted. Hang on, I thought. Wasn't he always on my case, telling me not to drink soda or eat candy? I didn't really want soda or candy anyway, but dutifully tramped off into the sweltering heat, wondering why he wanted me to amscray like that, for no real rhyme or reason. Besides, it was a lot cooler in the sanctuary than it was outside under a sun hotter than the Eye of Sauron.

When I returned, I noticed there were two other cars parked in front of and behind our shabby vehicle, cars with far finer pedigrees than ours. One was a Benz, black as venal sin, and the other a most excellent vintage white bathtub Porsche. For whatever reason, I was alarmed by them, girdling our jalopy the way they did. There was plenty of room to park up and down the street, so why make it impossible for us to squeeze out of our spot? Just seemed sinister to me.

Inside the church all was hushed other than men's voices coming from the basement office, softly distant as if they were murmuring in a mine shaft. Following my instincts, I sat on one of the wooden pews far off to the side and continued to work on my half-melted chocolate bar while waiting to see what there was to see.

I didn't have to wait long. A fellow in a tailored suit soon emerged from the doorway that led to the stairs down at the end of the nave, thickish leather briefcase in hand, and strode with presidential purpose along the far aisle toward the front door. I didn't stir or say a peep, and he didn't notice me as he passed by, his face an unreadable blank, just a man walking along minding his own. When he exited, a shaft of brutal silver daylight invaded the dark interior of the church long enough for the large oak door to open and close. Right after that, my father and another man I no more recognized than the suit that had just come up from the catacombs, in part because he averted his face, were talking about things that, try as hard as I could to understand, I couldn't make hide nor hair about. I do remember the man saying "Milton." But that was only because there was a skinny kid at school with that name, Miltie Milquetoast was his uninspired nickname, and he was always catching flak because of it. And as they walked down the aisle toward the door, their footsteps on the stone floor echoing more audibly than their voices, I swore I heard my father say, "...generous margins." Generous margins? Clueless as to what they were talking about and feeling a little weird that they were so close to me but thought they were all by themselves, I cleared my throat.

"Hi there, Liam," the reverend said in a very different, louder, more carefree tone of voice. "Give me a minute here, son," and with that he and his companion, who decidedly looked away so I could no longer see his face, went outside together, not saying a further word in front of me.

I smelled something was up. And if a smell could be deafening, that's the smell I heard. For one, it wasn't like him not to introduce me. He brought me up to be more polite than that, and even if I didn't always measure up, not by a long shot, wasn't it somewhere in the Bible that it was the parent's job to teach by example? Maybe not, but damned if this whole episode didn't made me nervous as a turkey on Pilgrim's day. It didn't help that when my father came back inside, he acted as if nothing out of the ordinary had even happened. Well, I figured, I had my secrets—ah, Amanda, I wonder if you knew how devoted I was to you back then—and I guess he had his. Just that those men didn't look like contractors here to discuss church repairs or even local businessmen offering loans or help or what have you. They and their cars were not, I believed, from our particular backwaters. Crocs from a different swamp, or I'm an alligator's uncle.

Back home, I wondered if the men at the church had anything to do with my parents' after-dinner wringing of hands. Beyond offering to look for a job and assuming they'd let me in on what was happening when it suited them, there was nothing I could do. So what I did was nothing, and put the matter out of my mind. My little brother Drew would ask me what was up, but I'm sorry to admit that I kept him as much in the dark as the progenitors kept me. I reassured him, my arm over his bony shoulder, which he disgustedly shook off, that just as they had persuaded me—not even slightly—that all was well, he should be persuaded, too.

"Kemosabe," I said, to his annoyance, "Life's tough. Chill, my man."

He ran upstairs to his bedroom and I didn't blame him. I knew more than he did, but because of that fact, I was even more confused than he. As I recall, I went up to my room, too, shut and bolted my door, and played on my Xbox all night. I hesitate to provide the name of the game, as it's not one I am proud of, but for partial disclosure, let it be said that pixilated blood was lost, virtual limbs were separated from their host bodies, and mayhem and madness blanketed the screen. In a healthy way, for sure. Getting my angst out, I suppose one could assert. Getting some balance back in my life. Sort of.

Rewind now back to present. My dad is dead.

My brother and I are fatherless. My mom's a widow. The First Methodist church has no minister. Winter's coming. None of these are even slightly good things. I liked it better when the reverend was around and I could be a friendly pain in his neck and my mom could feed him his meat, vegetable, and starch every evening, and our little corner of the world thrived on its trivial routines. At the same time, hard as it was to wrap my tired and meager brain around it, thanks to my father's bequest and the literary nougats I discovered inside those dusty Bibles, I was worth well over a million dineros. If there was ever such a thing as a silver lining on a cloud, this was it. Not even silver, a gold lining. I kept everything to myself but wondered why my dad, looking as haggard as our threadbare sofa, wasted so many evenings worrying about church finances when he had to have known that any one of these books would have bought him a new organ or paid for his steeple repairs. I wanted to shout "We're rich" to my mom and brother at the top of my lungs, but I knew I needed to stay calm, remain as stupid as I looked until I got a better handle on how my pater acquired these rare books and why he had been so worried about money during the last months of his life.

Whether from concern or lenience or distractedness or all three, my mother allowed me one last day home from school. I had told her I was feeling a little better, cough cough, but as it happened, a soaker of a rainstorm had settled in, driving the last leaves out of their trees and hammering against the window panes. If it had been nicer outside, she probably would have made me go. But since the weather was rotten and it was a Friday, anyway, she gave me a pass.

"Monday means you're back at it, though," she warned while stirring the hot oatmeal she was cooking us for breakfast.

"No problem," I said, sitting in my robe at the table, trying to appear chipper and under the weather at the same time. "And I'll get my makeup work going as soon as I can."

Oh, I was a regular valedictorian.

As it turned out, it was a good thing I stayed home that day since I had almost as many visitors as Amahl. Not three friendly kings but two men showed up unexpectedly, one in the morning, the other midafternoon.

I was upstairs documenting books when I heard the doorbell ring. Quickly replacing a slim volume by Samuel Taylor Coleridge back in its biblical hiding place, I cinched my robe, slid into my slippers, went downstairs, and opened the door. The detective, Reynolds was his name, stood there looking every bit the street thug once again, if this time showered and smelling of fresh talc. And, as before, I took his casual appearance to be a sign that he was good people, somebody I could maybe trust. Not that I was in a trusting mood.

"Hey, Liam," he said, as the chilly outside air blew around him and right through me.

"Hello, sir."

"Your mom in?"

"Not right now," I said with an unfeigned sneeze.

"Well, as it happens, I wanted to talk to you, too," he went on. "I see you're home sick, though. I can come back another day if that's better."

I should have said yes, but the words, "No, that's okay, come on in," flew out of my mouth instead.

We sat down in the living room. I knew the polite thing to do would be to offer him some of my mother's leftover coffee, given what a cruddy day it was outside, but kept my mouth shut. Sure, I kind of trusted him, but there was no need for me to roll out too big of a welcome mat. Besides, I didn't want him or anybody else messing with my inheritance. Money aside, I had gotten very possessive of my books just as, or so I'd started to believe, my father had.

Reynolds was speaking about how he was still on the case regarding my dad's death. "I seem to be the only one in the department who isn't convinced it was a hundred percent accidental. Coroner ruled it accidental. Prosecutor's office sees nothing in it for them to pursue a trip-and-fall. I got no leads, just a nagging hunch. Looks like it's only you and me thinking there might have been foul play," as he summed it up, an awkward smile very briefly complicating his face. Smile gone, he asked, "You still thinking, like the last time I saw you, that your father was the victim of a crime?"

"Maybe," I said, less sure now if the reverend wasn't the perpetrator of one, too, since I knew he hadn't enough dough on the up and up to acquire even one of the rarities hidden inside those Bibles upstairs, sharing shelf space with my innocent smut.

"You sounded a lot more sure the last time I dropped by."

I shrugged, feeling almost as guilty as if I had killed him myself.

"Well, since I'm here, let me ask what I asked your mom the other day. Have you had any visitors or phone calls that are out of the ordinary?"

Black sheep atheist though I styled myself, I thought the better of lying to a cop, even one who, like Reynolds, was nonchalantly dressed like a homeless man in fifty cent's worth of threads from Goodwill. Somewhere behind his rumpled sweater and ripped jeans there was a badge lurking, and my personal brand of anarchism only went so far.

"A guy did call looking for my dad. Didn't know he was dead, I guess."

"Did he say what he wanted?"

"Nope. And when I asked him his name and number, he hung up on me."

"You didn't tell him your father was deceased?"

"Not my job."

This made Reynolds smirk a little. "Figured he might give you a clue if you played dumb, eh? Smooth thinking, Liam. One of these days you might want to consider going into my line of work. Better watch out for my job."

I didn't want to insult him by saying that I'd rather be a blind garbage man with brain cancer and no legs than a police officer, so I said instead, "Well, the fish wasn't biting."

"You know what reverse dialing is? You try that?"

"I tried, but it was blocked."

"I have a question for you, Liam," Reynolds

said, shifting subjects as he shifted on the sofa, and his voice also shifted to a more buddy-buddy tone. "After your dad died, we looked through some of his records at the church just to see if anything was suspicious. You know, to see if he'd gotten any hate mail or stuff like that."

"No way," I said.

"You're right. We didn't find a thing. Your father was very well liked."

All this hollow pitter-patter was now making me antsy. It was my last day with the house all to myself and I still had a dozen Bibles left to open and catalogue, and though I didn't dislike Reynolds, he was getting on my nerves. I waited for him to finish whatever was on his mind.

"Well, since there really is no criminal investigation still going on—like you, I've got the day off—I don't have any legal right to ask you this and doubt if I could even get a judge to issue a search warrant, but I'm wondering if your dad had an office in the house here, as well as in the church basement?"

"Not really," I said, relieved. That was a pretty long windup to a slow pitch, and I was bracing myself against the possibility he was going to ask about my Bibles.

"I was just thinking that since you and I are the only ones who think there might have been wrongdoing involved, that if I could go through his desk at home—"

"Well, my mom's the one who did all the bookkeeping and I guess you could have a look at her stuff if you thought it was important. I doubt she'd care."

"If it's not a lot of trouble," he said. "I don't want to impose."

"No problem," I told the detective, grateful to accompany him to the downstairs family room, a corner of which doubled as my mom's study, because it led him to a part of the house that was in the opposite direction of my trove. Besides, even though he didn't really have any right to riffle through her papers, as he himself conceded, my mother, of all people, had nothing to hide. As I led the way down, I heard him breathing a little heavily behind me, and thought to myself he needn't be so excited about all this since I knew there was nothing to be found that would assist in his investigation. And yet, while I stood there shifting weight from one foot to the other while I watched him go through her files, I found myself feeling a bit annoyed that I'd allowed him access. What if he did find a misplaced piece of paper that might betray the existence of the rare books hidden upstairs? On top of that, long minutes were ticking by that might better have been spent doing my internet research.

I was right, however. He discovered not one thing worthy of pursuing further.

"I knew it was a long shot," he said, clapping his palms down on his knees where he sat on my mother's swivel chair, and rising to go. "I really appreciate your time and trust, Liam." As we headed back upstairs, he added, "We probably should keep this to ourselves, if that's all right by you."

"No reason not to," I said, having no intention of telling my mom anyway.

At the door he thanked me again, requesting that I get in touch if anything developed that I thought he might need to know.

"I'll keep an eye out," I assured him, then hacked out a cough that was almost as fake as my brother's had been a couple of days before.

"You take care of that cold, you hear?" he winked, handing me his card before sliding on his raincoat and leaving. I watched through the front door window as he lit a cigarette while ambling down our walk, then neatly tucked the match back into his pocket rather than toss it on the long wet grass that could have used one more mowing before the snow started.

That's one sharp hombre, I recall thinking.

Don't want to find myself on the wrong side of his good graces. Bad for health. The fact was, since the reverend didn't keep a separate office at home and they found nothing among his papers at church, I'd figured there were no papers to be found, period. That this assumption would prove to be way wrong was probably what got me started, in my tender middle teens—Amanda, how I missed having all my spare time to think of you and you only—on my first ulcer.

Why wrong? Because less than an hour later, having discovered a 1843 first edition, first issue of Dickens's *A Christmas Carol* with hand-colored illustrations by John Leech, and another early sixteenth-century Aldine title by Lucretius that needed more research but looked promising, I opened one of the last of my smuggler's Bibles to find not a rare book but a sizeable stash of cash, about thirty grand, and a bunch of handwritten notes. The tidy wad of barely-circulated hundreds, held together with rubber bands, I put back where I found it, my fingers gone a tad numb. The notes, however, I spread out on my bed with utmost care. I knew what I had stumbled on even before I started combing through the receipts to sort out which ones went with which books.

Hurrying, I glanced at the treasures inside the

remaining Bibles, jotted down my own notes about their authors, titles, dates, and so forth, then moved the trove of Holy Books into some boxes where I used to store my childhood comics before I sold most of them for enough to cover my Xbox acquisition. I cleared out the back of my disorganized warehouse of a closet, carefully stacked the boxes there, and proceeded to hide them under layers of wrinkled clothes, sports equipment I never used, a sleeping bag, piles of stuff it would take a team of archaeologists to dig out. The only Bible I kept out, besides the one my preacher father actually used to read when he wasn't busy hoarding high spots of Western culture, was the one with the cash and paper trail in it.

Now, I always thought it strange that my father, who had a booming sermonizer's voice on Sundays, possessed such dainty old lady's handwriting. Just never made sense to me. Be that as it may, while his lion's roar may have been gone, his little kitty claw marks remained on many of them.

Like some born-again bean counter, I started going through the slips of paper. At first I was frustrated to see some of the notes about prices were coded. What, for example, did $RLTAS and $VEASS possibly mean? My heart sank. I saw reassuring names like Milton, Dryden, Swift, Poe, scattered here and there in the thicket of scrawl. Some of them were in my closet and others listed were not. When I happened to uncover a scrap that had been wadded up like some spitball with the word "$Revlations" penciled on it, I understood after a bewildered moment it was, eureka, the reverend's price code. An ironic one, too, if you stopped to think that it was not meant to reveal a thing. Seemed he had chosen a book of the Bible in which, when he dropped one "e," each letter could stand for a number, one through ten, and who'd be the wiser? Well done, pop, I thought proudly as a wave of missing him spread through me like the fast fever of a real cold, not my pretend act. It made me shiver to think of him somehow managing to assemble these books, to keep his doings so tight to the vest, or vestments I should say, and then the doorbell rang for the second time that day. Sensing this hoard of notes was almost as valuable as the books themselves, I stuffed them back in the hollow with the money and hid the Bible under my pillow. I had to figure that even if my room was searched by an alien strain of vampire stormtroopers they wouldn't deprive a sick, mourning boy of his bedtime copy of the Word of God.

Leery by now of unexpected visitors, I peered out an upstairs window and saw, to my astonishment, the same black Mercedes I'd seen that freakish hot August day, parked right in front of our house. Was there any way this could be good? No, I didn't think there was any way this could be good. But I couldn't hide inside the house like a book in a Bible for the rest of my life hoping my father's rare book contacts—and I was sure, Amanda, that's who this was, wishing like crazy I could disappear in your warm, dreamy embrace—hoping they would leave me alone now and forever, Amen.

The doorbell rang a second time. Nothing ventured, nothing gained, and all that. I slunk downstairs and opened the door. Middle-aged man wearing the most dapper raincoat I ever laid eyes on with its collars turned up. He had a salt-and-pepper moustache, steel-blue eyes, a learned face. City-looking, natty urban.

When he asked if my father was home, very polite and well-spoken, I recognized his as the voice on the phone from before. I also knew, seeing him there, beads of water trickling off the brim of his chic brown fedora, that he really and truly didn't know that the person he was asking after was no longer with us. Which meant, of course, that this wasn't the murderer.

"I'm afraid my father passed away two weeks ago." I didn't need to use any of my pathetic acting skills for it to be clear what I said was true, and that it upset me.

The quick look of shock that swept across his face was more proof that this guy was out of the loop on my dad's status and troubled by the news. "I hadn't heard, been overseas on business. I'm terribly sorry for your loss. He and I had arrangements, you see, to meet and—I don't know what to say."

"It's wet out there. You want to come in?"

"Well, just for a moment."

We stood in the hallway, him dripping, me shivering.

"I think we met once before, in the church some months ago," he said. "May I ask how your father passed away? It must have been a sudden illness. He seemed healthy when I saw him last."

"We weren't introduced," I said, to clarify. "But yeah, we saw each other once. My dad died of a concussion. He fell down the stairs at church. They say it was an accident."

Took me long enough, but only then did I notice he had his leather briefcase with him.

"You don't seem too sure it was. An accident, I mean."

With that, he suddenly sounded concerned.

My first impression that he was clean as a fresh-washed window might have been wrong, I thought. "Me, I'm just a kid, so what do I know." Bread on the water, again.

"You seem like a pretty smart kid to me. None of my business, but I assume you've spoken with the police about your suspicions."

"Oh, sure. The detective who's looking into it stopped by this morning to go over a few things with me."

"Did he. Well, let's hope he gets to the bottom of it. I admired your father very much and we shared some of the same interests. In fact, I'd brought him something he and I had discussed before I went abroad," he said, lifting the brief case slightly. "But I suppose it doesn't matter now."

That statement obviously left me in a quandary because I both knew and didn't know what was in the briefcase. Had my father's books so taken hold of me, so seduced me like they had him, and probably this gentleman whose name I still hadn't asked for, fool that I was, that I was dying to know what he had brought? I couldn't recall ever being in such a helpless bind. If I had even the slightest hint of a moustache, not the convincing sculpture of whiskers that crowned this man's upper lip, I might have had a fighting chance to say, Hey, I know about the books. What've you got there? Something in vellum? A duodecimo or, like, a royal quarto? More Boethius, more Lucretius? But I sensed I hadn't a fighting chance.

I did go ahead and venture, "If it's a present or something, I could pass it along to my mom for you," hoping to coax some information out of him.

The wheels in his mind were turning. If he were a cartoon character, the illustrators would make it so you could see inside his head, pistons cranking, smoke billowing in the air like the gray ghost of a cauliflower.

He floored me when he finally said, after, I swear to every angel fluttering around on butterfly wings in heaven and every devil who ever poked a pitchfork in a sinner's behind, what had to have been a full minute, "It's not a present. Your dad wanted it for a—friend of his who was going to buy it. It's a little complicated."

The brief hesitation that ballooned before the word "friend" meant it wasn't a friend. I was young, yes, but I wasn't born yesterday. Curious before, now I was riveted.

He continued, the wheels in his mind still turning, "I'd give it to you but the problem is, you wouldn't really know what to do with it."

"How complicated could it be?" I asked. I mean, I loved my dad but doubted what he had been up to here wasn't beyond my own modest abilities.

"Your name is Liam, isn't it?" he said.

"Yes."

"Well, mine's John Harrison. I'm wondering if you'd mind if I took this coat off for a minute?"

"Oh, sure," I said, feeling that things might be drifting my way.

We sat, as if some movie director told us to and we were obedient actors, just where Reynolds and I had earlier. Harrison settled his briefcase between his polished black wingtip shoes.

"Did your father ever share with you his passion for books?"

Unbelievable, I thought. Was this guy really going to tell me what was what?

"For the Bible, sure. After that, not so much."

"He liked other books, too. You like books, Liam?"

"They have become of real interest to me recently," I said, mangling my English in an effort to sound sophisticated.

"I happen to think that would make your father extremely proud."

"What sort of work do you do, Mr. Harrison?" I asked, hoping to turn the spotlight away from me. I tried to make my question sound chatty, not pushy, but even before he answered, a raft of other questions flooded my mind. How did you know my father? Why all the secrecy around these books? Who was that other guy with the white Porsche? If my dad was pushed down those stairs, why was he pushed? What the hell was going on here?

"You can call me John if you like, Liam. What I am is a librarian," he said. "Like you, I've loved books ever since I was a kid, and when I grew up I figured the best way to be near what I loved was to work in a building filled with books."

"Makes sense," I said, ignoring his patronizing tone, waiting for more.

"It can be a little boring at times, but the job has its benefits."

"That's probably true of all jobs, no?" I could tell he was weighing something most important to him, so didn't stress over it myself but did have to wonder when he would get to the blasted point.

"Listen, Liam," said Harrison, or, that is, John, after another of his pauses, this one briefer than the others. "How good are you at keeping secrets?"

I thought of the more than sixty Bibles buried in my bedroom closet, thought of my beloved Amanda, thought of the often daydreamy life I led behind my locked bedroom door, and answered, "The best."

"Good. I kind of thought so," he said. "Your father, being a man of cloth, probably taught you what the phrase 'to take a leap of faith' means?"

"Sure, I know what that means."

"All right, I'm going to take a leap of faith in you, okay?"

"I'm chill with that," I said, wishing immediately I had expressed myself less like some wannabe hip-hopster and more like a responsible grownup.

"Good," he continued. "Have you ever heard the word 'deacquisition'?"

"No, sir, I haven't."

"What about 'deaccession?'"

I didn't know that one, either, so he explained what they meant and went from there to tell me a lot of other interesting things. The more I spoke with John Harrison, the cooler, or rather more estimable, he seemed. I could see why my father enjoyed his friendship, or working with him, or whatever they did together. We conversed for an hour, him treating me more like an adult than anybody had in a long time, actually ever, telling me a little about a world I might never have imagined existed before I inherited my trove. Once I got the gist of what he was saying, and hearing the clock strike four, I told him my mother and brother would be coming home pretty soon, and he left after shaking my palm-damp hand, taking that book with him for safekeeping just for a few days, never knowing that it probably would have been just as safe if not safer in my tenderloin clutches. Unless what he let me in on was a pack of lies, which it wasn't, I just felt it in my bones, the reverend had quite an interesting double life going on here for the past several years. On the one hand, it fried my circuits to think of him, my bike-riding, sermon-preaching dad, as an under-the-radar outlaw. On the other, I found myself weirdly proud that he'd led a whole clandestine life nobody might have guessed. That he was so squeaky clean made it possible for him to take a walk on the wild side. Yes, my mind was blown but, at the same time, I was deeply inspired. Looking back, I see that day as the one when I became, for better or worse, a man.

True to my word, veritable poster boy of godless integrity that I was, I didn't let on to my family about my second visitor that Friday, although I did tell my mother that the detective had dropped over.

"He have anything concrete to tell us?" she asked, filling the kitchen cabinets with cans of soup and vegetables after finding a place for a carton of milk in our fridge, which was already overstuffed with casseroles and pot pies that neighbors and congregants had dropped off after the funeral. To her credit, mater had kept up the same dinner regimen that kept pater so hearty during their years of marital solidarity. If meatloaf, mashed potatoes, and canned peas were good enough for a man who ministered to hundreds of unwashed souls over the years, and secretly collected and fenced rare books—I hadn't known, until Harrison told me, that the word "fence" had another meaning beyond chainlink and pickets—then loaf, spuds, and mushy peas were good enough for me.

"Not really," I said, neutral as a glass of water. "He told me that the rest of them he works with say it was an accident. Guess they don't have any clues." I was about to add that maybe we should consider suing the church since there was a little lip on the third step down on which he might have caught the tip of his shoe. But then I realized we would pretty much only be suing ourselves. Besides, who knows whether the insurance was all paid up. Just seemed like a dead end in every sense.

"Well, then, I wish he'd stop coming around and stirring up bad memories."

"I hear you, Mom. But his intentions are good," remembering that line about how the road to perdition is paved with good intentions. She was right. Especially now that I knew what I knew. It was going to be best if Reynolds did back off. If I stuck to that old bit about *An eye for an eye, a tooth for a tooth*, it could wind up being my eye and my tooth that might go missing. I didn't know whether or not my poor father tripped and plunged down the stairs all on his lonesome. Point was, either way he was gone and there was no getting him back. And, like it or not, the less the police looked into his death, the less the chance they would uncover his curious secrets. He was beloved by his tightfisted flock, I thought. Let him stay beloved.

"I think Liam did it," my little brother, who will never get a blue ribbon for sanity, offered up to no one in particular. Three years my junior, he might as well have been a decade younger the way he acted sometimes.

"Hush your mouth," said my mother, a nice little flash of anger stoking her words.

"Yeah, zip it, Kemosabe," I concurred.

"Stop calling me that," he countered.

"Calling you what, Kemosabe?"

"Both of you. Stop it right now."

The soundtrack for dinner that night was all forks and knives against plates, glasses of juice being gulped and set back down on the table, highlighted by an occasional sniffle from my stuffy nose. Looked like I was finally coming down with the cold I had been faking all week, comeuppance from a wrathful deity no doubt. I went to bed early, no Xbox, no tube, no *De rerum natura*, and slept in a pool of sweat until late morning the next day.

"You okay in there?" my worried mom asked, knocking lightly on my door.

"Be down in a minute," I said, then lay there for another half an hour thinking about how much I missed Amanda, since the church was closed until a replacement minister was found, but also about Harrison, who'd given me his cell number. I don't think he could believe it any more than I did, that he basically offered to let me consider picking up where the reverend had let off. Obviously my dad had been a fence for the ages, since it didn't look like Harrison was taking his business elsewhere. Although, I had to wonder, maybe there weren't any available elsewheres. Or, at least, elsewheres that could be so covert and trusted.

"You're young to be doing this sort of thing," Harrison had said toward the end of our meeting, or whatever it was, almost as if he was thinking out loud. "But there's a matter of some urgency involved here with finishing up the prearranged transactions—"

I felt proud that I was suddenly asked to be part of a transaction. Transactions were never kid stuff. The word was just too big and stately to have anything to do with playing marbles or touch football or comparable baloney.

"—that were already in process before your father passed. Claude ought to be in touch in a matter of days, and there's quite a lot of money at stake for all three of us."

Again, I loved feeling I was a part of a sophisticated gang or ring where each of us depended on the other and the lucre was flowing like spring melt.

"So if I could trust you to help complete the deal, I'm sure your father would've been grateful. And it'll be some decent walking-around money for you. Just that you can't let anyone notice, or ever tell anybody, ever, is all."

"You can trust me," I said, and meant it.

Whether or not the reverend would have

been grateful, it didn't seem to me to be very hard work, and its shadier side attracted the anarchist in me. Harrison would give me a book to transfer to another man, this Claude guy, who would give me an agreed-upon amount of money, which I'd pass along to Harrison after taking for myself what he called "the courier's percentage," and everybody was happy as proverbial clams. Since Harrison couldn't safely get directly in touch with Claude and finish things up on his own—they didn't want to meet or talk or know each other at all—it was up to me to bridge them.

"Why not?" I had asked, in all innocence.

"It's better for you that you don't know why not, Liam," Harrison explained, or rather didn't explain. "'Why' is a word best stayed away from."

Never liked that word, anyway, so it was easy enough for me not to ask.

"How do I reach this Claude person?"

"You don't," said Harrison. "He reaches you."

"Well, how will he know if I have something for him?"

"He won't, not exactly. You either will or you won't have what he wants," Harrison said. "Thing is, it all runs along more smoothly than you can imagine. Your father always told me that Claude is a pleasant fellow, and I think you'll agree that your father was a good judge of character."

Fair enough, I thought, not sure whether my dad was a good judge of character or not. Steering clear of the word "why," I tried to push the river a little more. "Does Claude own a white Porsche, like one out of a sixties movie?"

"You know, Liam, I admire your curiosity. I admire your pluck. It's impressive in someone your age. The answer to the question is not necessarily. And the answer to your next question, if I'm guessing it right, is that it's best you don't know at this point. You okay with that?"

"All good," I said, more and more liking the craziness of what I was hearing here.

The warm smile that dawned on Harrison's face made me feel ten stories tall. How I wanted to know what book it was he had in his briefcase. What century, who the writer was, what the binding looked like, all that interesting stuff. No doubt it was worth some righteous dough, but strange as it sounds, that came in kind of second for me. We—my family and my dad's old church—needed money, for sure. But the book itself, the physical object, and my response to it, had a quality that couldn't be put into words, even if I had a thousand years to try. The closest I could come, then or now, was love. I'm not the sentimental kind, not much anyway. But love was what I felt, both pure and simple, and impure and not so simple. No, it wasn't the same love I had for Amanda—I felt no deeper love for anyone or anything—but still, it was a rich, growing love for these old leather-bound antiquarian Xboxes, vellum-covered TVs with programming by Boethius and his excellent crew of fellow scribes caught immortal on the page. How I wanted to tell Harrison right then and there I was all in. Instead, I kept my cool. He would find out soon enough. Smart son of a gun probably already knew he had a partner in me.

Besides, the words my mother told me not long after my father's death came back verbatim, sharp as the razor I'd just started using on the feathery whiskers on my chin, firm as the smooth cement floor on which my dad cracked his skull. "Now you're going to have to be the head of the family," she had told me, "and take your father's place in whatever ways you can." I had no idea what that might require of me when she said it. But times had changed, quick as a slip on a step, and life was upside down and inside out. I couldn't afford to sit around wishing things were like before. I knew what I had to do in order to measure up. Knew what kind of man I had to be.

With that decision, my course was essentially set for many years of my young life. To cut away the fat and the gristle and carve straight to the meat of the matter, I went for it. Harrison met me briefly, furtively, near an elementary school playground, to pass along the book he'd brought for my father—this time in a nondescript brown paper bag—after phoning to find out if I was up to the task after giving it a little thought.

"Yes, sir," I told him. "Proud to have the opportunity."

I fulfilled my obligations well enough that I continued as go-between, wearing my father's sometime mantle with pride, caution aplenty, and in the growing knowledge that any college degree I might have pursued was trumped by the symbiotic education I was getting by handling, researching, and reading these books. Fatuous or gushy as it might sound, they inspired me to learn more than I ever might have learned in academia.

What astounds me, looking back at those callow days, those yearning-to-learn days of methodical madness, those good boy-bad boy days, me watchfully passing back and forth the rarest of rare books and the coldest of cold cash, is that the Harrisons and Claudes of this world would take a chance on an underage, unproven cadet. See, the way I figure it, if my saintly father had been selected as the perfect recruit to be a part of this operation of liberation, as they saw it, or, more like it, pretended to in order to maintain their dignity, their integrity, and all that, then I, his eldest, but an innocent youth, was an even better go-between and minor partner in the scheme.

Wisely, I never spoke with Harrison about the genesis, as it were, of my involvement in my father's onetime sub rosa business. All we discussed was books, payables, receivables, and a number—there were many more than just that one Claude—of code-named collectors and dealers. Claude? As it turned out, all of our buyers were named Claude. Because transactions were cut in cash, I never saw a personal check, never saw a driver's license or any other form of identification. I didn't know and I didn't want to know the real names of these fellow addicts. Claude was a perfect moniker, I thought, since, I mean, please, was anybody in the history of the world ever really named Claude?

And in my father's gone but not forgotten footsteps, I wound up keeping some of the books I should have passed along for my commission but could not part with. All more or less on the up and up, for the record, since I paid Harrison for what I kept, cash out of my savings from the middleman fee, and just told potential buyers that the book wasn't available after all, instead offering them one of my father's books I didn't care to keep any longer. Sure, I ran into disappointment now and then, but, knock wood, not suspicion. Between the reverend's sterling reputation among the various parties and my own winning youthful earnestness—weird that the less innocent I was, the easier it became to make myself look innocent—all moved forward without a hitch. At the same time, I didn't let my immediate family, or anyone else, know about my trove. It was a challenge, but though I didn't increase the number of volumes in my little collection, I systematically increased its value. By the time I was in my early twenties, still living at home after Andrew himself had headed off to college, or, well, community college, my smuggler's Bibles housed rare books that were worth upwards of two and a quarter million dollars in retail value. That family acquaintances thought I was an underachiever who sadly lost his footing after his father's death was flat-out wrong but worked sweet as punch for me. I bagged groceries at the local store and eventually worked my way up to manager, just for show, but was making clandestine gelt hand over fist, or maybe hand under fist would be the more apt metaphor. Either way, an illness, an obsession, a passion—forgive me, my Amanda—for which there was no clear cure had taken me over.

I did figure out ways to funnel money to my mother for household expenses over the years, sometimes considerable amounts that surprised her, covering my tracks by lying that I had hit lottery jackpots, a grand here, a few thousand there. She bought it since she didn't have much choice, and was grateful in her poker-faced way. I also clenched my teeth and tithed to the church, whose new pastor delivered sermons that moved me not one bit more than my father's had. But I attended services anyway, partly to accompany my mom, partly to make Harrison happy, since he wanted me to maintain as virtuous an image as possible. But mostly because Amanda, who worked as a bank teller during the week and, having moved on from her Sunday school teaching, sang in the choir on Sundays, even taking over conducting whenever the regular director—Mrs. Thoth, a nice lady with a pear-shaped face, who had worked with my father for many years—was absent. She, Amanda I mean, had grown more and more fine as the years went by. Age became her, at least to my Amanda-consecrated eye. In all truth, she was a beautiful young woman with a warm smile and ready laugh, a prize many would consider worthy of far better than the lanky likes of me. But that wasn't a roadblock that could stop my heaven-ordained pursuit.

If I was Dante, Amanda was my Beatrice. After some initial hesitation on her part, we began taking walks after services. Walks that were, for many months, opportunities to get to know one another. I think she began to see me less as the minister's son and more as a real person, well-meaning if quirky, devoted if shy—shy at least around her. As for me, my adolescent longings were eclipsed by her simple presence, the presence of a truly decent human being. We spoke of our love of music, hers, and books, mine. She started reading some of the masterworks of literature and philosophy that interested me most—some of which I secretly owned as first editions—as well as a few novels by Lawrence and Henry Miller that I considered classics. And I went over to her house to listen to recordings with her of her favorite music. I might never have guessed that, along with Bach, Mozart, and Beethoven, her most cherished composers were Maurice Ravel and, yes, Claude Debussy. That she also liked Prince made me fall for her all over again.

Somewhere in one of my smuggler's Bible books, there must be written a theory that would explain the things that came together all at once during that misty May of my twenty-first year. Well, not the things themselves. But how those things were connected by taut invisible strings which that gnarly puppet master known as god had decided in his great wisdom to pull. I can try to explain, since god certainly would never bother and even my beloved Boethius might not have been equal to doing.

Amanda had floored me when, the year before, she allowed me to kiss her during one of our walks. A long, tender kiss beneath a secluded tree, a kiss I had never believed in my heart of hearts would ever translate from fantasy to flesh. Who knows, maybe rubbing elbows with my learned librarian friend Harrison—who I suppose had become a bit of a father figure for me—gave me an air of sufficient sophistication that Amanda, over half a dozen years my senior, considered attractive. Perhaps having more money stashed under a scrap heap of laundry in my closet than all my neighbors had, added up times two, afforded me an adult confidence. Maybe it was because I actually finally succeeded in reading Nabokov and even tried my hand at understanding paperback translations of the works I owned in Greek and Latin, French and German. Who knows. Why ask why?

What happened was that our Sunday walks developed into shared evenings, dinners and movies, a train ride now and again into Manhattan to go to Carnegie Hall and hit some museums, and it wasn't long before she and I were spending lots of time together, more than I had ever hoped for back in my lusting tenderfoot years. In all seriousness, I was astonished to find that my daydreams, my wet dreams, my longing boyhood dreams were not wasted on some kind of delusion, and that the girl I thought I loved back in my youth turned out to be the woman I truly loved later. Cynical and defensive as I had been when I was younger, I always figured what I was experiencing was pure fiction, not the real deal like my father's death, my mother's decline. Such joy was, I knew, dangerous since it was fragile and rare. As fragile and rare as any of my hidden rarities.

Because the reverend had always adored Amanda, never privy to my filthy thoughts, of course, it was easy for my mother to embrace her current presence in my life. Deep down, I think my mom would have given up a dozen of me and my brother to have had just one daughter, not that I could blame her, for all the minor scuffling trouble Drew and I brought into her life over the years. A daughter would have made her time with my starchy pater a little more gently rumpled, and I mean that in a good way. Well, to some degree, Amanda filled that daughterly role for her, helping her make a pot roast after church some Sundays, advising her about hair colors when the old lady wanted to get a dye job, stuff like that. And it couldn't have made me happier for both of them, since it turned out Amanda's mother was no picnic, another story for another day. My courtship, a term my mom actually pulled out of the mothballs of her mind to describe my dating Amanda, was going better than I might ever have imagined possible. Not only did we say we loved each other, but Amanda claimed she liked me more than anyone she'd ever met.

She one day said it like this. "I've always had a secret crush on you, the handsome son of the handsome preacher. I guess you could say I've always loved you from afar. But I really like you, too. Silly as it sounds, I'm in like with you."

I don't think I could honestly claim that anybody I'd ever known, Harrison included, my family included, might be able to make the same statement. Oh, that Liam fellow? Now there's someone I truly and sincerely like. Forget about it.

During one of our Sunday afternoon suppers, I think it was lamb chops and new potatoes on the table, the doorbell rang unexpectedly and I went to answer.

"Hello, Liam," Reynolds said. "How's all and everything?"

Acting unsurprised as I could manage, though he probably wouldn't have been surprised to see me surprised since he hadn't stopped by in years, I told him all and everything was fine, thanks.

"I was just driving by the house and thought I'd check in on you and your family."

No choice but to let him in. "That's really nice of you."

"Who is it, Liam?" my mother called from the dining room.

"Detective Reynolds is here," I answered, praying she wouldn't ask him to join us.

"Ask him on in to join us if he'd like."

"No, tell her that's okay, Liam. I don't want to bust in on Sunday dinner, especially unannounced like this."

Not wanting to shout back and forth, I said to him, "That's all right, come on in why don't you. I'm sure she'd love to say hello. My girlfriend's here, too."

"You have a girlfriend now, do you? That's great," he said, but didn't budge an inch farther into the house. "I hate to be rude, but it was you I wanted to talk to if you had just a moment." He looked at his watch, a fakey-fake gesture that sent up, as my father used to put it, all the red flags in China.

"Hang on," I told him, then went to the dining room to say the detective wanted to have a word with me privately and I'd be back right away.

"Something about your dad?" my mother asked, setting her fork down on her place, voice fluttering like a buckshot bird falling out of the sky.

"No idea," I said, and looked at Amanda, who had picked up on my mom's nerves and clearly shared her concern. "Don't worry. Just go on eating and I'll see what he has to say."

Back in the foyer, Reynolds tipped his head to suggest we step outside. I grabbed my slicker off the coat rack and walked with him into a mist so fine that it looked like it was raining upwards instead of down. Parked at the end of the walkway was that same dark blue unmarked Chevy he was driving when I first met him.

"Guess you like that car," I said, breaking the ice, if ice it was between us that caused the silence.

"You got a good memory, Liam," he said with

a light laugh. "I'm still wondering why you didn't become a detective like I thought you might. You have all the smarts it takes to solve mysteries. God knows, you probably have more smarts than the job requires."

I thought it best not to thank him.

"Plus, it might beat working in a grocery store."

"Maybe, maybe not," was all I could think to say. It annoyed and worried me that he knew where I worked, since I had never once seen him in our aisles.

"So, it's been quite a while since we talked about your father, how he passed."

"Yeah," I said, as we turned onto the sidewalk and ambled down the street away from the house.

"I hope you don't mind me bringing it up again, hope I'm not opening old wounds."

"I guess not," I said, looking away from him toward the window of our neighbor's house next door. Why was it their curtains were always drawn, no matter what the weather?

"Well, I didn't want to get your mom's hopes up but I think we may have a possible break in his case. After all this time, it doesn't happen that often. I mean, for a cold case to suddenly get warm again."

That same strange feeling of guilt, like I had killed him myself, came over me then. It wasn't a feeling I liked one bit, a ridiculous sensation since I was sitting right there with my little brother and mom when the accident happened. But I felt it anyway. I just hoped that Reynolds, who was sharp as ever and curiously intimidating, couldn't feel it, too.

"How so? What happened?"

"There's a man, his name doesn't matter, who passed away a few months ago, died of natural causes. Lived with his wife on the Upper East Side of New York. An advertising exec, did well in his career, made good money."

"Doesn't sound like the kind of guy who would push a minister down some stairs."

Reynolds paused, took in a deep breath, exhaled. "Well, you're right. At least partly right. You see, this man was a collector. Collected all sorts of things from coins and stamps to paintings and books. He had great taste, to say the least, and as it's beginning to come clear to those who were tasked with probating his estate, it looks like his taste went way beyond his income, which was already pretty hefty."

I naturally had already made the possible connection, but said, doorknob dumb, or trying to be, "I'm not seeing what this has to do with my dad yet."

"Well, I'll get to that now. You see, it looks like he was working with some dealers, suppliers of fine art stuff, not all of them totally legit. For instance, turns out one of his best paintings, a portrait of some girl by Degas—"

Reynolds mispronounced the name so it rhymed with Vegas, but I kept my tongue glued to the roof of my mouth. I didn't like the direction any of this was going.

"—was stolen from a museum in Austria. And there were other items, not by any means all of them, by the way, that seem to have come from institutions here and there. So, here's the bit that bothers me regarding your father. His address and phone number, both at the church and your house, were in a little book this collector kept in a wall safe."

"That's nuts," I said.

"It is nuts, you're right. Especially since, so far as the authorities working on all this have been able to determine, a number of the other names and contact info listed in his book could be traced to dealers in coins, stamps, art, and various collectibles like that. Now some of them have checked out, but others are under investigation. And as you can imagine, all the assets of the estate are frozen until his collections can be gone through with a fine-toothed comb to see what's what."

I made my first mistake ever with Reynolds when I said, "I'm lost here."

"Well, I have to doubt that, Liam," glancing over at me as the heavy mist turned to light drizzle. "I can imagine you wouldn't want to think your father, being a preacher and all, could be caught up in anything even slightly illegal. But there are some questions about why he was in this man's address book that will have to be answered at some point. Whether your dad found himself involved in any of this, which I seriously doubt, by the way, isn't really my ballywick. But his death was and is."

I said nothing, not wanting to say something wrong. Tongue glued, tongue glued.

"Did you ever know your father to be interested in collectibles at all?"

"No, sir," now finally lying.

"People used to like stamp collecting a lot. My grandfather had a humongous collection of stamps and when he passed away, we had them appraised, since he had always talked about how valuable they were and that we could all retire on it. Well, turned out his stamps were basically worthless, moneywise. The whole value was in his enjoyment cutting them off of envelopes and buying them out of catalogues for nickels and dimes."

"I never saw my father collect anything"—no, I didn't slip up and say, except for Bibles—"and that even included collecting enough during services to keep his church fixed. He and my mom sat around all the time worrying about money. Collecting would have been about the last thing on his mind."

"Well," Reynolds said, taking me subtly by the elbow and turning me around with him to head back toward my house. "If anything comes to mind, anything at all, that might explain what your dad's info was doing in this man's possession, would you let me know?"

"I doubt I'll come up with anything, but you can count on me to call if I do."

"You still have my card?"

"I'm sure I do."

"Look there. You have the instincts of a collector as well as a detective," he said, the wiseass. "Let me give you another one, just in case."

"Thanks," I said. "You sure you wouldn't like to come in for dessert? Amanda, that's my girlfriend, makes a mean pecan pie."

"I'll raincheck that, but next time for sure, okay?"

"You got it," I said, and shook his hand with the best smile I could summon from my slim arsenal of smiles. I turned to head back up the walk as he opened his car door. "Am I supposed to keep all this stuff to myself? Should I ask my brother anything?"

How I hoped he would say yes even as he said, "No. Just keep it to yourself for now."

"What am I supposed to tell my mom when I go back in?"

That did seem to throw him off a little. Hadn't thought that part through, I guess. "I don't know, just say I wanted to check in, catch up a little for old time's sake. I'm sure you'll come up with something."

My thoughts chasing in circles, I used Reynolds' excuse on Amanda and my mom, having no better bright idea.

That night, in bed, having driven Amanda home, my worries only darkened. I wanted to call Harrison but feared that my phone might be tapped. I wanted to get my Bibles and their precious charges to a safer place than my closet, but where in the world could I stow them until any danger passed? Above all, I desperately wanted not to believe my father had been pushed down those stairs to his death because of some sort of book deal gone sour. This last desire was the toughest of the three because it never seemed more plausible that this was exactly what had happened. I went through the faces of all the Claudes I had met over the years, wondering which Claude might have been this attorney who was fishier than sushi, but had no way of sorting out one from the next. That was how it was meant to be, of course. Just for occasions like this. If nobody was connected with anybody else, then nobody would take a fall simply because somebody else did. No game of dominoes here. And no one was ever supposed to have written anything down, which is why the reverend had his cost code and the Claudes were all blank slates. I never asked Harrison where he had deaccessioned all these books from, what library's rarely visited shelves were a little emptier than they had been, their once-upon-a-time presence having been erased forever, like some calculus equation a stupid schoolboy solved incorrectly on the chalkboard. The only common link was, like my father before, me.

What I did early the next morning, dawn failing to slice through the dense overcast, was— Amanda, my saving grace—I drove over to my girlfriend's and asked her if she could take the morning off work.

"You seem serious today, Liam. Are you all right?"

"I am serious, and I am all right. Better than all right, better than I've ever been."

We strolled to a pretty little park, one we liked a lot, not far from Amanda's apartment building. The sun hovered above us, white as a flag of surrender, trying like anything to break through the clouds. The bench we found was, like the rest of the park, empty and wet from last night's rain. I took off my jacket and wiped dry a spot where we could sit, holding hands. Damned if Amanda didn't look lovelier than ever, the shadows on her face softened in the pearl-gray light. Rotten as my juvenile thoughts about her over the years had been, I realized they'd brought me to this place, me sitting with her, not with some lewd made-up story about her but Amanda herself. When I asked her, "Manda, I love you so much, always have, and I wonder if you would marry me?" and she answered without hesitation, as if she'd pondered the possibility for a long time, "Nothing would make me happier, Liam," I felt the sun break through and even though it didn't it may as well have, given how full of warmth and light I felt. We kissed each other, held each other close, and as I walked her back so she could get ready for work, we agreed that we would tell my mom that evening and afterwards go out to dinner somewhere special and celebrate. Caviar and champagne, the works.

Back home, I got busy. The Bibles were already in a half a dozen weary boxes that had come from the church way back in the dark ages. A couple had maybe housed quart bottles of grape juice for all I knew, but their labels had all peeled off so the boxes were nondescript, old, and, I hoped, untraceable. I slipped contractors bags around them, to keep any rainwater off and to make them all the more anonymous. Like some criminal, which I suppose I was in fact, I made myself more anonymous too, by putting on my father's very unhip clothes, including a plaid sports jacket that was so hideous even he had never worn it. Up and down our street there were, as almost always, zero signs of life, but I made quick work of it anyhow. My heart heavy as a cobblestone, my eyes welling and blurred, I loaded the boxes into the trunk of my car—my mother still used the old wagon to ship herself to and from her lousy job, so I used our other one, another junker I had bought with my so-called lottery winnings that was good for getting from here to nearby there and nothing more. Our pathetic village library was too close to my neighborhood for comfort—I had considered the town dump, but terrified as I was about getting caught I couldn't bring myself to desert my precious trove there—so I drove a few hamlets over to a larger town, traveling through rolling terrain highlighted by ruined farmhouses and sad swayback horses standing in mucky fields.

At one point, seeing I was driving erratic as hell, I had to pull over to catch my breath and try to calm down. I sat there, muttering an apology to my father, and gazed out at one lone red horse that stood nearby, chewing away, his jaw zagging sideways, his big chocolate eyes trained warily on me. He looked like a mythic sage who had lost his train of thought. When I found myself starting to apologize to him, too, I snapped to, thinking, You have no choice here, Liam, no free will. Get this done already.

The library might as well have been a mortuary. Lights seemed to be on but there were no other signs of life. I parked in back of the building, a yellowish brick structure which, like my father's old church, had seen better days. Underneath a rusting metal eave at the top of a short flight of cement steps, I stacked the boxes against the rear door, which looked to be a delivery entrance. Let me confess that I fought back tears as I looked at the black plastic-wrapped boxes piled there, feeling like a bereft parent who was deserting a newborn on the doorstep of a church or police station, abandoning the child, one whose care and upbringing were beyond the realm of possibility, to the mercies of strangers and fate.

Head downcast and hands in pockets, I walked away from my trove with more grief than could ever be written down and printed in some damned book. As I climbed into my car and turned on the ignition, I leaned my forehead against the steering wheel and felt a breach had opened in my heart that I knew would never mend, a wound that meant I was losing my father all over again. But I was a man now, soon to be a husband, maybe even a real father one day, a father who would never abandon his kids, and to be a man meant sometimes you had to leave certain things behind with the hope that better things lie ahead. That's what I was telling myself, like some fool idiot saying a prayer, until I heard a knock on the car window that caused me to jolt upright in the car seat with the violent abruptness one experiences when waking from a nightmare.

I turned to see my father peering in at me, his face so very familiar with a look both furious and—how could this be?—friendly. My dead father viewed through the shimmering and unsteady lens of my tears, my father who I then recognized was in fact Reynolds staring in at me, his hoodie cowling his visage like a demonic monk. Stunned, speechless, I saw him flick his fingers toward his chest, that vintage gesture used by cops to indicate, Would you mind stepping out of your car, sir?

Defiant, or so I hastily tried to be, knowing my eyes must be ringed pink and wet, I rolled down the driver's side window, saying nothing.

"So, Liam," he said, after glancing to his left and right before he rested his forearm on the door. "What's the word?" The playful frown on his unparted lips and the way he tilted his head with the cocky confidence of one in full Machiavellian control boded nothing but trouble. Once my friend, or so I had naïvely believed, Reynolds had developed a knack for asking questions that left me speechless.

I had no word for him, I realized. "I'm not sure what you mean," I ventured.

"Well, let me try to help you out. What I mean to say is, I was wondering what's in those boxes over there?" he asked, snapping his head back in the direction of the library while continuing to level his unblinking gaze at me.

Any joy or sadness I had experienced that

day, from proposing to Amanda to the necessary decision to abandon my trove, came to a quick terminus. I swear I could literally feel the blood drain from my face.

Reynolds was still speaking. "Don't you want to get a receipt from the librarian if you're going to make a contribution of books? It's tax deductible, you know."

With one last pathetic grab at saving the situation, I said, "I don't make enough money to need a tax deduction. Was just thinking they could use some Bibles."

"Well, that's interesting, Liam. You know why?"

"No, why?"

"Because I was just thinking that I myself could do with reading the Bible more often. Working in my field, I encounter so many bad guys that sometimes I feel they have a negative influence on me. I worry now and then that I might turn into a bad guy myself if I don't watch it. Some Bibles might be just the thing. Some remedial reading, isn't that what it's called?"

I waited. His frown rose into a half-smile now.

"Let me ask you a question, you mind?"

My engine was still idling. I thought if I just dropped into gear I could end this puzzling discussion here and now. But did I really want to go to jail on the same day that the love of my life had accepted my proposal of marriage?

"My strong impression, watching you from afar—or, well, maybe not from so afar as you might think—is that you like those Bibles, even need those Bibles, as much as I do. I also suspect that you know far better than I do about how to mine them, if I can make a little pun, for their true value. Being the son of a preacher, and all, I mean. You agree with that, in principle?"

I squinted and nodded.

"Which is not to say I haven't been given alms now and then to keep prying eyes, so to speak, at bay. And I was happy to oblige, you know, even way back when, until I began to realize, not long before your father passed, what a pittance was being tossed my way."

Was I hearing right? I wondered. Was I just witness to a confession?

"I don't know about any of that," I said.

"Well, that's all right, you don't really need to know more. But look here, meantime. What do you say we get those boxes out of the wet weather, throw half of them in the back of my car"—and he gestured across the street behind me toward the vintage white bathtub Porsche parked there; I suppose I should have been more horrified than I was—"and the other half in yours, and get out of here before whoever is supposed to be running this silly library comes back and claims your donation. We can work out any details about our Bible studies later. What say?"

"Do I have any choice?"

Reynolds paused just a fleeting moment before answering, "None that I can think of, offhand."

Back home, after disposing of my pater's eccentric clothes and burying my remaining half of the trove in the back of my helter-skelter closet, not even bothering to see if I ended up with the Voltaire or the Shelley, the Donne or the Pindar, I opened an account at Amanda's bank with my so-called lottery winnings. Time had come for me to confess to my fiancée I'd been lucky scratching tickets over the years. She forgave me in the car, driving over to tell my mother the happy news of our betrothal, but also was practical enough to realize the money represented a nice nest egg with which to start our fledgling marriage. I swore—not on a stack of Bibles, no, but I meant it anyhow—that I would never gamble again. Both god and the devil, gamblers themselves, could verify I haven't, if only they existed.

For a handful of months after that encounter

with Reynolds, a blessed oasis of time, nobody named Claude called me, or Harrison, either. The Claudes I didn't much miss, but one day, feeling a nostalgic longing to hear Harrison's voice, see if he was all right, see if any more books might be coming my way—*our* way, if one counted Reynolds—I called him from the anonymity of a pay phone downtown. It rang a few times before a recorded message came on and a monotone disembodied voice told me this number was no longer in service. My fellow congregants in the religious order of literary rarities had disappeared as if they had never been more than a crazy figment of my imagination. This hiatus soon enough came to an end. One day, a colleague of Harrison contacted me to say he had something either I or Harvey—Claudes were now known as Harveys, to me an equally preposterous moniker—might find of interest. Were it up to me and me alone, I would have respectfully announced my retirement and bowed out. But I had other mouths to feed than my own and, in all honesty, my bibliophilic malady might have been driven by fear into remission, but I could not fairly claim to be cured of it.

Reynolds showed up periodically, asking me if I had read any good books lately and, out of habit or lunacy or simply to remind me he held the dangerous upper hand, inquired if I'd had any contact from anyone suspicious, anyone who might have been involved in the reverend's death. Some days I told him I hadn't and that seemed good enough for him. On other days, I let him know that indeed I'd had a visitor, a fellow book lover, and handed him an attaché case containing either money or, if he liked, a new acquisition—or should I say, rather, deacquistion. Amanda, who knew nothing about any of these activities, of course, thought it was kind of Reynolds to take time away from his demanding job to stay in touch with me, and even come to our wedding, which took place on a sunny Saturday afternoon in my father's beloved old church. It was not her problem that I had become his minion, as it were, one who secretly chafed at the bit and bided his time.

And speaking of time, I had to wonder how many months or even years might pass before the good detective, my objectionable colleague, might make a fatal misstep on a staircase somewhere and plunge, a look of malign astonishment frozen on his face, to the unforgiving floor at the bottom. If and when it happens, will he even have time to curse my name, or my father's? No, I think he will not. His end is foretold in the Bible, after all, in Leviticus and elsewhere, and just because I remain at heart an unbeliever, I recognize that it is a book that holds many valuable truths and worthy mandates.